Karen McCombie

is the bestselling author of the *Indie Kidd* series, as well as other fiction for children and teenagers. She used to write for magazines *J17* and *Sugar*. Karen lives in London with her husband, small daughter and one fat cat.

Lydia Monks

won the Smarties Prize for *I Wish I Were a Dog*. She has illustrated many poetry, novelty and picture books for children, including *Little Big Mouth* for Walker Books. Lydia lives in Sheffield with her husband and children.

For the always lovely
Ella (Bella) Gregory
KMcC

574846

First published 2009 by Walker Books Ltd
87 Vauxhall Walker, London SE11 5HJ

2 4 6 8 10 9 7 5 3 1

Text © 2009 Karen McCombie

Illustrations © 2009 Lydia Monks

The right of Karen McCombie and Lydia Monks to be identified as author
and illustrator respectively of this work has been asserted by them in accordance
with the Copyright, Designs and Patents Act 1988

This book has been typeset in Granjon

Printed and bound in Great Britain by
J F Print Ltd, Sparkford.

British Library Cataloguing in Publication Data:
a catalogue record for this book is available from the British Library

ISBN 978-1-4063-1189-1

www.walker.co.uk

KAREN McCOMBIE · LYDIA MONKS

I Spy a (not so) White Lie

WALKER
BOOKS

The teeny-tiny... what, exactly?

It was spookily quiet in our house.

And eerily dark, in the kitchen at least.

Scritch-scratch!

I stopped, and looked around for whatever was *scritch-scratching*.

Scritch-scratch!

In the gloom, I could make out a cardboard box on the kitchen worktop.

Scritch-scratch!

Tip-toe-ing over, I got closer and

closer to the box, and the strange scritch-scratching noise.

Scritch-scratch!

Holding my breath, I folded open one cardboard flap, quiet as I could.

SCRITCH-SCRATCH!!

With my heart pounding, I peeked inside, and saw... **a ghost!**

A very teeny-tiny, weeny, white ghost, blinking back up at me!!

"Oh, hello, Indie! I didn't hear you come in," said Mum's voice suddenly. "Did you have a nice time at your dad's?"

Mum was at the kitchen doorway, drying her hair with a big pink towel. There were probably bits of hamster bedding in the shower plughole now.

Having a mum who is manager of an animal rescue centre means that you get **a lot** of hamster bedding in places you wouldn't expect, like the CD player and the letter-rack.

"Yep," I answered her, closing the cardboard flap quickly so the teeny-tiny, weeny, white ghost didn't swoooooooosh out.

I'd had a very nice time at Dad's this Sunday. Me, Dad and my stepbrother

Dylan had watched *Kung-Fu Panda* on DVD, while Dylan's mum Fiona used us as fancy-flavoured popcorn testers. (It's great having a step-mum who has to invent new recipes for her cookery column in the local paper.)

"So you saw my note alright?" Mum asked.

"Uh-huh," I answered her. It had been pinned to the banister. It said,

Don't put light on in Kitchen!!
Don't open blind !!!!!

That might have sounded quite stern, but was written in our lodger Caitlin's purple nail varnish so didn't look very stern.

9

(Mum obviously couldn't find a pen before she went to have her shower. She's a bit scatty when it comes to practical things. Last week, I gave her a permission slip for a school trip. Just before I handed it to my teacher, Miss Levy, I saw that Mum had scrawled 'Worming tablets x 3 cartons' in the gap where she should have signed 'Lynne Kidd'.)

Scritch-scratch!

"Are you hungry? Shall I put the tea on soon?" asked Mum, acting as if the scritch-scratching was a completely normal kitchen sound, like dripping taps and humming fridges.

"Um, no, I'm fine," I replied. My tummy was stuffed with peanut-butter flavoured popcorn.

"We'll leave it for a bit, then," Mum murmured distractedly, turning to go.

Scritch-scratch!

"Er, Mum – why is there a teeny-tiny, weeny, white ghost inside this box?" I asked her.

"Ah, yes. That's a baby barn owl. I got an emergency call earlier to say someone was bringing it in to the centre," Mum explained. "Thought I'd take it home and keep an eye on it…"

OK, that made sense. Mum often took things – furry, feathery, squeaky or squawky things – home from work to look after.

Our normal pets (three dogs, one squashy cat, six-and-a-half fish) were pretty used to sharing the house with newborn hedgehogs and giant land snails and stuff. They'd be fine with a baby barn owl. Still, it was bound to be nocturnal… which made me ask an important question.

"Is the kitchen going to have to stay dark?" I asked, wondering if I'd need a torch to search out my Rice Krispies in the morning.

"Nope – I'm going to turn the shed into an aviary," said Mum. "Speaking of birds, what did Mrs O'Neill say when you dropped off the birdseed this morning?"

Arghhhhhhhhhhhh...!!!

Mrs O'Neill was our old lady neighbour.

She had the flu.

She had run out of birdseed for her budgie, Archie.

Mum had asked me to drop off a packet of seed this morning, before I caught the bus to Dad's.

But this morning, my head was full of **fun stuff** instead... my best friend Soph had phoned to tell me that her mum had won a **raffle prize.**

13

The prize was for a family of five to go to a new Mexican restaurant on the High Street, this Friday.

Soph's parents said she could invite me and our other best friend, Fee. I didn't even know if I'd like Mexican food, but Soph said the waiters all waved maracas and for pudding they did ice-cream sundaes with marshmallows, which was good enough for me.

So with a head full of maracas and marshmallows, I'd walked right past Mrs O'Neill's and got straight on the bus to Dad's...

OOpS.

Right, so the obvious thing to do was say, "Mum, I forgot!! Sorry!!"

But instead, I…

a) got myself in a complete flap,

and

b) came out with something really, really, REALLY stupid.

A lie

"Mrs O'Neill?" I gabbled nervously. "She… um… she said thanks very much and, er, everything."

Aargh, what had made me do that?

I never lied! (Unless it was a white lie, like the time I told Dad he looked fine, when he was actually dribbling out of the corner of his mouth after a trip to the dentist.)

Boy, was I glad that the kitchen was dark and Mum couldn't see me blushing. How **stunned** and **shocked** would she be if she knew I was fibbing?

I was **stunned** and **shocked** enough at myself. **Help!** How was I going to get out of this? And how would lying help poor, starving Archie?!?

Eek, eek, eek... I squeaked silently in a muddle of panic.

"Good!" said Mum, as the phone started ringing in the living room and she went to answer it.

Yesss!! If Mum was on the phone, I could zip over to Mrs O'Neill's and back without her suspecting a thing.

It was going to be OK, I realized with a mega-dollop of relief. Mum wouldn't know anything. Archie wouldn't starve. I could undo this stupid, thoughtless, dumb little lie as quickly as I'd made it up.

Hurrah, phew, etc...

"Just going out to see the dogs!" I gabbled, grabbing the birdseed out of my bag.

My dogs had ignored me when I'd come home; Kenneth and George had been lying on the lawn, eyes locked on Dibbles, who was busily eating the rubber

Bart Simpson dog toy I got him yesterday with my pocket money.

But now that Dibbles seemed to be full (there were only a few rubbery Bart crumbs left on the grass), all three dogs welcomed me with barking loud enough to be heard on the moon.

"WOOF! WOOF! WOOF!!"

"Stay!" I ordered them, nipping out of the gate.

George bounded straight over it, and Kenneth reached a paw up high enough to unclip the latch so that he and Dibbles could waddle out after me too.

"WOOF! WOOF! WOOF!!"

Oh – there in Mrs O'Neill's living room window was… well, Mrs O'Neill. She was staring out to see what all the **woofing** was about, while talking on the phone.

A prickle of panic fizzled up my back.

Flipping around, I stared back at my own living room window and saw Mum, staring out, while talking on the phone.

I got a sinking feeling. She was talking to Mrs O'Neill, wasn't she?

She'd just found out that I hadn't taken the birdseed over this morning, hadn't she? **"WOOF! WOOF! WOOF!!"**

So there I was, frozen on the pavement, with three bouncing, barking dogs and a giveaway bag of birdseed in my hand.

I couldn't have looked more guilty if I'd had a giant neon arrow above my head with **"LIAR!!"** written on it in flashing multi-coloured lightbulbs.

I couldn't have felt more awful if I'd sat on my cat Smudge and squashed her.

Oh, how I wished I could swap places with that teeny-tiny barn owl baby, and fold myself up to fit in that cardboard box in the kitchen.

That would be so much better than being caught out as a **big fat fibber**...!

2
Feeling blaaahhhh...

DRINGGGGGGGGG!!!!!
As we walked towards the classroom first thing on Monday morning, I felt Fee rub my back, the way mums do when they're trying to get their babies to burp.

I don't think Fee was really trying to to get me to burp,

it was more that she was doing a 'there-there-it'll-be-alright' rub.

I didn't feel very alright, though.

As for Soph, well, she gave me a soppy, sympathetic look, as if she'd just heard that all my pets had run away from home or something (which is obviously quite hard to do if you're a goldfish).

But no pets had run away. Here's what was making me feel so **blaaahhhh** today: I'd just told my friends about my dumb lie about the birdseed and my disasterous punishment.

"It's only Monday. Your mum'll change her mind by the end of the week!"

Soph suggested.

"No, I don't think she will," I said sadly.

Mum had been pretty definite yesterday afternoon. There were to be no maraca-waving waiters and no ice-cream sundaes with marshmallows for me this Friday. **Sighhhhhh**...

I was bluer than blue. My heart felt all bruise-y with guilt and my head felt fuzzy with **weirdness**. Everything since yesterday's fib felt **weird**.

My mum was **weird**, 'cause she was all stern and disappointed, instead of *dreamy* and *ditzy* like usual.

24

The house was **weird** 'cause Caitlin –
who is our nineteen-year-old lodger and
my childminder – was away in Scotland
visiting her family.

No Caitlin meant **weird** silence; she
was always playing rock songs (**weirdly**)
on her (**weird**) didgeridoo.

And now school felt **weird** 'cause this
sure looked like my classroom but there
was someone I didn't recognize sitting at
the big table at the back where me, Soph
and Fee always sat.

I swivelled round, thinking that in my fog of **weirdness**, I'd taken a wrong turn into next door's classroom by accident.

Then I really did cause an accident.

Well, a mini people pile-up.

"Indie!" said Miss Levy.

At first, I couldn't figure out where her voice was coming from, till I realized she was splatted on the floor.

"Sorry, Miss Levy! I got in a **muddle**!"

I said quickly, hurrying to help her up.

Out of the corner of my eye, I could see the girl-who-shouldn't-be-sitting-at-our-table still sitting at our table, staring at the *muddle* I'd just made happen.

Of course, lots of kids in my class were sniggering now, especially Simon Green. Simon Green is one of those boys who really, really likes it if people do dumb things. Specially if it involves someone getting hurt.

"No harm done, Indie," Miss Levy said breathlessly, as she got up. "But you really should be more careful, shouldn't you?!"

"Sorry, Miss Levy," I said in my best sorry voice.

"Well, I always trust you to be good role model for others, Indie," said Miss Levy, sort of frowning and smiling at

me at the same time. I didn't know how she did that. If I tried to frown and smile at the same time, my face would look like very strange indeed, and probably scare my dogs.

Then Miss Levy looked a bit worried. I think it was because I was sort of crying.

"Don't worry, Indie!" she said quickly. "I'm not cross with you!"

I never liked it when Miss Levy told me off because I liked Miss Levy a lot. But I think I was sort of crying because she'd just spoken about trusting me, and that reminded me that Mum certainly didn't trust me anymore.

My mum just thought I was a **big, fat fibber.**

"Come here, Indie," said Miss Levy, leading me over to our table. "I want you and the Sophies to meet someone!"

Oh… the girl at our table.

"Girls, this is April, who starts in our class today," I heard Miss Levy say.

I couldn't see April too well because my eyes were still a bit cloudy with tears. But through the haziness, she seemed small-ish and blonde-ish.

"Hi!" said the girl who looked a bit like the baby barn owl (but without a beak and claws, as far as I could make out).

"Hello!" said Soph and Fee together.

Aarkkk!

I squawked, 'cause I had a trying-not-to-cry lump in my throat.

"Girls, can you look after April and help her settle in?" Miss Levy asked us.

"Yes!" said Soph and Fee, all excited.

I didn't say anything, 'cause I thought I might **'Aarkkk!'** again.

"Right, I'll leave you to get to know each other for a couple of minutes before register," said Miss Levy, giving my arm a gentle squeeze before she walked away.

"I'm Soph!" said Soph to the girl.

"I'm Fee!" said Fee to the girl.

"I'm April!" said the girl to my friends, but not so much to me, since I hadn't introduced myself to her (I was too scared she'd think my name was **'Aarkkk!'**).

"Where have you come from?" asked Soph, gazing at April as if she was a pop star, or made of chocolate and gold.

If I'd been April, I might have said 'Space!', just to get everyone laughing. But instead, April said the name of a primary school I thought I'd heard of, on the other side of town.

"It was OK, but my dad said this school was better. And I had loads of friends and everything but I think it'll be fun to have new friends too," said April.

Fee opened her mouth to say something, but April started talking again.

"My last name is Furneaux, which is French, but from a long time ago, because nobody in my family is French!"

"Oh!" Soph jumped in. "I'm half–"

Soph's mum's French and her dad is from Somalia, which I think is quite interesting. April didn't seem to think so.

"Anyway, my middle name is Joni after a singer my dad loves. He wanted to call me Joni for my first name but my mum wanted April because that was the month I was born in!"

"Oh, real—" Fee tried to say.

"I was nearly March, though, because I was only born five minutes into April. Wouldn't it be funny if my name had been March?"

Soph and Fee giggled. They didn't seen to mind that April kept talking right over them. I thought maybe that was a little bit **rude** and **annoying**…

"Everyone! Quiet, please!" Miss Levy called out. "It's time to say a big hello and

Parrrp!

welcome to our new girl, April!" April smiled. Simon Green made a sound with his hands like a **big fart.** Everyone (except April and Miss Levy and me) burst out laughing. April's smile went wobbly.

Uh-oh. I immediately felt mean for thinking so badly of her when she was brand new and probably a little (or a lot) nervous.

I was practically as bad as horrible Simon Green.

34

Yep, I didn't like myself very much right now: I was **mean,** as well as a **fibber.**

In fact, if I was me, I wouldn't want to be my friend right now...

3

All about April

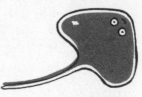

"**MMMM, MMM, MMMM!!**" mmm'd April Joni Furneaux.

She was acting like our Monday school lunch was caramel and fudge, followed by toffee, instead of plain old lasagne and peas, plus a muffin.

36

Maybe April was still nervous, but the way she described stuff was **waaaaay** over the top.

"Your hair... it's like a fairy princess's!" she'd whispered to Fee, when we were supposed to be doing maths.

(Fee had gone all shy and pleased and ended up tangling her pencil in her **curly-wurly** hair.)

"**WOW!** You should go on a TV talent show!! You'd definitely win it!!" she'd gasped, when Soph showed her a few of her Irish dance steps in the playground at breaktime.

(Soph got carried away with the compliment and Irish-danced sideways into something she shouldn't have.)

"Oh my goodness! Take it away!! If I ate like one crumb of that, I would totally die!" April had squealed, pointing to the quarter of a Snickers bar I was offering her as a pre-school-lunch snacklette.

(I was trying to show myself that I wasn't mean – how was I to know she had a deadly peanut allergy?)

We'd found out lots more about April at break, not just that nutty chocolate bars were toxic to her (shame).

We'd found out that…

• her old teacher was called Mrs Cheer but was grouchy

• her best friends were Ria and Terri-Ann and they were gutted that she had left her old school

• her favourite colour was pink (all shades except the colour of candyfloss)

• she once got a temporary tattoo of a skull and crossbones on her arm but it wouldn't wash off for five weeks

• she used to be great at gymnastics till she swung off the parallel bars at a funny angle and lost her nerve

• she'd been on the London Eye six times

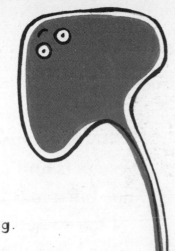

- she didn't like aquariums because the rays spooked her out with their tiny eyes and one bit her once, and...

- flossing made her gag.

Phew.

Stuff April found out about us: **zero**.

Strangely, Fee and Soph didn't seem to mind that April was doing all the talking and all we were doing was nodding and smiling a lot.

But I kind of did. Maybe it was because my neck was starting to ache with all the nodding and my over-used smile was sagging.

Anyway, now – in between '**mmm's** April was telling us about her house.

She was using a lot of soooooo's to describe it.

"My house is soooooo cool."

"Indie's house is cool too! She has all these pets and animals and stuff in it!" Soph burst in.

I felt myself blushing, all pleased and embarrassed.

"And she has this crazy childminder who has amazing punky clothes and plays the didgeridoo!" added Fee.

I gave a shy smile. It was really nice that my friends liked me and my house and my pets and my crazy childminder enough to talk about it to the new girl.

April seemed to listen – blinking her big baby barn owl blue eyes – then gave a little shrug, as if Soph and Fee had just been speaking in Mandarin and she hadn't a clue what they were on about.

Or maybe it just meant, "So what?".

Or maybe I was just being **mean** (again), 'cause once April started talking, Soph and Fee were all fascinated and charmed by her (again).

"Anyway, get this: my bedroom is soooooo big, I can have six girls for a sleepover, easily!"

"**Oooh!**" (That was Fee.)

"And I have this white, wrought iron bed with a white net curtain with sparkly sequins all around it and it is soooooo beautiful."

"**Wow!**" (That was Soph.)

"I've got my own TV and DVD and Sky Plus, and the screen is soooooo huge!"

"**Really?!**" (Fee)

"And for my last birthday, my dad bought me this mini American-style pink fridge, so I could have my own juice and snacks in it for when friends come round!!"

"**cool!!**" (Soph)

I opened my mouth, thinking that maybe I should say something, but I couldn't think what.

And I couldn't say what I was thinking, which was

I'm jealous

Oh, yes, I was **jealous**, as well as **mean** and a **fibber. Great**...

Loose bits and flatness

My ends were loose. Or I was at a loose end, or however that dumb saying goes.

I was back at home after school, thinking about my loose bits, and feeling **flat**.

I knew a big part of the **flat** feeling was 'cause of the new girl at school today. Well, 'cause my best friends seemed to think she was so ace, while I didn't and wondered why.

A smaller bit of the **flat** feeling was 'cause of the whole **fibbing** thing with Mum yesterday. Though with Caitlin still away, Mum had picked me up from school in the Paws For Thought Rescue Centre van, which was quite cool. And she was back to her usual smiley, *ditzy* and forgetful self, which was cooler still.

But she hadn't forgotten about grounding me this week **(boo!)**...

Whatever, as soon as we got in the house, Mum vanished.

Well, OK, she was out in the shed/look-alike aviary with Casper.

(We'd called the baby barn owl 'Casper' after Casper the friendly ghost. I loved that film when I was little, though I did sleep with my head under the duvet for three weeks after I first watched it.)

I'd wanted to help with Casper, but Mum had said no, 'cause he shouldn't be around people too much or he'd never manage to go back in the wild.

That was fair enough. But left **mooching** around on my own in the house, I realized I was at a loose end and felt flat. Oh, and fed-up.

"Keep busy; that's the way to take your mind off the grumps!" Dad once told me when I was moaning to him on a very rainy Sunday afternoon.

He was right – that day, he went and made an indoor assault course out of sofa cushions. Then he timed me and Dylan running around it, and it was brilliant fun (my neat-freak step-mum Fiona was luckily out shopping, or she'd have fainted at the sight of all that cushion mayhem).

So what with my loose ends, flatness and fed-up-ness, I reminded myself to get busy.

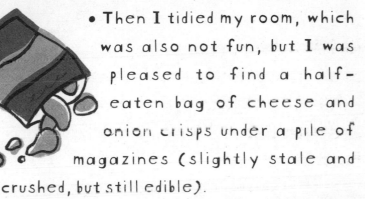

• First, **I** did my homework, which wasn't exactly fun, but felt good to get out of the way.

• Then **I** tidied my room, which was also not fun, but **I** was pleased to find a half-eaten bag of cheese and onion crisps under a pile of magazines (slightly stale and crushed, but still edible).

• **I** played tag with the dogs, till one by one they got bored and went for a scratch and a snooze.

• **I** tried to interest Smudge the cat in a game of chase-the-string, but she ignored me and carried on with her impression of a gently snoring furry cushion.

ZZZZZZZZ

49

• I watched the goldfish for a while, but my big, looming face must have been too magnified for them, and one by one, One, Two, Three, Four, Five and Five-and-a-half all skittered off to hide behind the plants with our very shy angelfish, Brian.

• I went into Caitlin's room, stepped into her platform trainers, and wobbled over to look at her scary coloured nail varnish collection – then decided to leave when I nearly fell back onto her didgeridoo.

50

• Finally, I remembered something mum had asked me to do – sign a card for Rose, the receptionist at the Rescue Centre, who was leaving this week.

I found the card on the kitchen table. It had 'Sorry You're Going!' written on it in goofy, multicoloured letters. Inside, lots of the vets and vet nurses and kennel assistants had written sweet and funny messages.

I bit the end of the pen and thought about what to write. Then I got it:

Dear Rose
I will miss you giving me chocolate biscuits when I'm waiting for Mu

I stopped there, noticing something odd out of the corner of my eye.

Dibbles was hovering.

Not in mid-air, of course. Sort of standing, but looking like he'd been about to sit down and something had stopped him.

Maybe his legs had seized up. Or his brain. (He is **adorable** but not very clever.)

"Are you OK?" I asked him, laying down the pen.

Dibbles looked up at me with one eye. (The other one was looking somewhere else. That happens sometimes with Dibbles.)

He opened his mouth, as if he was going to say something. **cool!** I thought. **A talking dog!**

But, instead, he barfed…

Well, cleaning up dog sick consisting mostly of chewed-up bits of Bart Simpson was one way to keep busy I guess, but I didn't like it much. In fact it made me feel more fed-up than ever.

I decided to phone Dad for a moan. Maybe he'd have another good idea about how I could cheer up.

Yep, that was the answer I got when I phoned Dad's number.

I knew Dad and Fiona would act like regular human beings and say "Hello?"

when they picked up the phone, so that meant it could only be one person.

"Hi, Dylan," I said to the silence.

"I got Gold level at school today 'cause of my weather project," Dylan said back.

Dylan is nine and very smart in some ways and very *goofy* in other ways. Let's just say he would not get a Gold level in having a conversation in a normal way.

But sometimes that's fine. It meant I could just say what was on my mind without faffing around with lots of "How are you?"s or whatever.

"Cool. This girl started at school today and I'm not sure what I think about her," I told him.

"Why not?"

I suddenly wondered if Dylan and his sideways way of looking at things might help me work out what I did think about April.

"She just talks about herself all the time."

"What does she say?"

"Well, this morning she told us about her huge house and all the amazing stuff in it." (That's when I felt **jealous** of her.)

"Then this afternoon, she told us about her dad, who looks like George Clooney."

(Still **jealous**. I mean, my dad's great, but doesn't look like a famous movie star one bit.)

"Then she told us that her step-mum is really mean, and so is her younger step-sister." (I felt **sorry** for her then, same as I did when Simon Green did the farty noise with his hands at register.)

"Oh, and I nearly forgot – she's said she could die if she ate my Snickers bar." (That's when I felt **bad** about nearly killing her.)

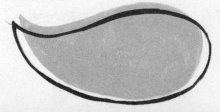

While I was in splurging mood, I wondered if I should tell Dylan about the birdseed and the fibbing and everything.

But the fact that he was saying a whole lot of nothing kind of put me off.

"So, what do you think?" I asked him straight out.

"I think she might be an alien."

"Excuse me?"

"Well, where has she come from? And why can't she eat normal earth food, eh?"

oh, dear.

"Uh, Dylan, I think I hear Mum calling for me," I lied (easily, since I was such a natural fibber). "Speak to you later…"

Amazing.

Thanks to a **mad** conversation with my step-brother (who was more like an alien than anyone I knew), I now felt **confused**, as well as **jealous, mean** and a **fibber**...

5
The trouble with stepfamilies

It was Tuesday.

There are lots of rules at our school. Not just on a Tuesday; for all the days.

Here's one. Actually, here's a whole bunch:

- No running in corridors
- No litter
- No chocolate in lunchboxes

- No mobile phones
- No chewing gum
- No sitting on the top of the climbing frame
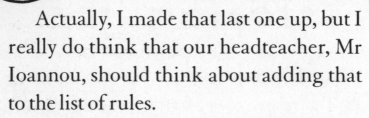
- No lauging at Simon Green's stupid jokes because it just makes him do them more

Actually, I made that last one up, but I really do think that our headteacher, Mr Ioannou, should think about adding that to the list of rules.

As for the other rules, well, they're all **true** and **fair** (except maybe for the one about running in corridors; it is dangerous, but can't be helped if you badly need the loo…).

And the no-chocolate-in-lunchboxes thing… well, people definitely don't have chocolate in their lunchboxes, but they, er, may have them in their jacket pockets at breaktime (hello, yesterday's chocolatey-nutty bar).

But apart from running when I need the loo and sneaking a Snickers into my pocket occasionally, I am very good at sticking to rules.

I was even sticking to the no-sitting-on-top-of-the-climbing-frame rule.

Mainly because there wasn't any room for me.

"Y'know, she hardly ever talks to me, she just leaves me notes," said April, her arms folded across her chest, sounding **resentful** and **sad**, and looking even more like Casper the baby barn owl, perched up there.

She was telling us more about her **wicked** step-mum, who sounded like she might be a cousin of Cruella De Vil. **only meaner.**

"But that's awful!" gasped Fee. "What does your dad say?"

"I can't tell him. He was so upset when Mum left, and so happy when he met Carla… Well, I just don't want to make him unhappy. Not again."

"Aw!!!" sighed Soph.

From my down-below position, I saw her wrap an arm around April's shoulders.

"You are so sweet! But you're not happy, so that's not fair!" said Fee, wrapping one of her arms around April's waist.

I think I should have been feeling really bad for April, but instead, all I could think about was the fact that she wasn't holding on, and if I reached up and gave her a tap on the feet, she'd swing forward off the top of the climbing frame and fall face first onto the squashy rubber matting.

Maybe she'd break into tiny glass pieces, or ooze green slime or burst into flames. That way, it might prove Dylan's nuts theory that April was an alien.

Of course, what it would actually prove was that I was a deeply horrid person, so I didn't do it. ('Cause I am honestly not a deeply horrible person, cross my heart.)

"What sort of things does your step-mum say in her notes?" asked Soph.

(Can I just say again that I am not a horrible person? I might have THOUGHT about tipping April Joni Furneaux off the climbing frame, but I would never in a million, billion years have actually done it.)

"Um, stuff like… 'Sort your room out now!' and 'Do the dishes!' and 'Tidy up all your sister's toys!'"

"No!" said Fee, taking her turn to gasp. "But why should you tidy up all your sister's stuff? I mean, she's only your step-sister!"

"Yeah! That's not even a real sister!" Soph chipped in.

When Fee and Soph said that, it made me go a bit wibbly inside.

I mean, my family broke up and then came back together in a different way (eventually), which was OK.

And maybe it took me a long time to get to know my step-brother Dylan properly, but nuts as he was, I liked him a lot.

"I have a step-brother called Dylan, and he's cool!" I chipped in, hoping Fee and Soph would add, "Oh, yeah! Of course!" since they hang out with Dylan loads of the time.

"Yeah, but he's not horrible, like April's step-sister," Soph said instead, looking sympathetically at April.

April smiled a sweet, sad smile.

"And I have a step-mum, and she's cool too!" I blurted out next, thinking of Fiona, and her excellent food experiments.

I mean, it's not like I would ever be mega-close to Fiona – not as close as to Mum (obviously) or even Caitlin (who was my buddy, as well as lodger and childminder) – but she was fine. A bit manic about crumbs and pet-hair and cushions-being-used-in-assault-courses, but fine.

"And does your step-mum always spoil her own daughter and ignore you?" asked Fee, ignoring me down on the ground.

"Absolutely! Daisy always gets what she wants. She is such a spoilt brat!" said April, rolling her eyes.

OK, so now I was feeling odd.

I was feeling odd 'cause...

1) How come April was making out like she was the Cinderella of her family when yesterday she'd been boasting about the size of her bedroom and everything in it?

2) Everyone on the climbing frame was making out that step-families were a bad thing when they weren't necessarily, and...

3) Two of those everyones on the top of the climbing frame were supposed to be my best friends, though they were acting like what I said didn't matter.

Actually, come to think of it, I wasn't feeling odd – just downright grumpy. **Seriously grumpy.**

"So where's your mum, then, April?"
I asked, suddenly wondering why – in
all her chat-chat-chatting – the new girl
hadn't talked about her 'real' mother very
much.

"She lives in Wales. But she phones
and calls me all the time. OK?" said April,
glowering down at me.

Which was quite a surprise, since I'd
started to think I had turned invisible.

"OK!!" I said grumpily back, which
made Soph and Fee frown down at me.

uh-oh.

It was only Tuesday, and now I was
grumpy, as well as **confused,
jealous, mean** and a **fibber**.

What a lovely week I was having so
far.

Not…

6

Funny frowns from Fee

Before break on Wednesday, I looked at Soph and Fee's chairs and convinced myself they were definitely a few centimetres closer to April's chair than to mine.

During break, I got roped in by Mr Ioannou to be a playground buddy and help a bunch of five-year-olds do a skipping game. It was such a **laugh** (specially when we all got tangled), that

71

I forgot all about
the seats-closer-to-April thing,
which I'd probably made up anyway.

After break, I walked into the classroom, planning on being all mature and asking Soph about Friday's Mexican meal, and trying not to sound all small-kiddish and disappointed that I wasn't going to it.

Yeah, that was till I saw Soph and Fee pull their seats around so they were sitting either side of April.

"Um, what are you looking at?" I asked, noticing that my so-called best friends were gazing down at something April was showing them.

"Photos from Disneyland Paris," said April, not even looking up at me. "That's me just after I'd been on Space Mountain! See, Soph?"

"Space Mountain? I've heard of that! It's the rollercoaster that goes practically supersonic fast, isn't it?"

"Mm-hmm," said April, nodding at Soph.

"But don't you have to be a certain height to do those big rides?" I asked, remembering watching some travel show once featuring a thing about Disneyland Paris.

(Caitlin had felt sick just watching the Big Thunder Mountain ride, and Kenneth had **Mee-hooowwwwlllled** along to the theme song they kept playing, *When You Wish Upon A Star*.)

"I'm tall enough," said not-very-tall April, shooting me a look like I was trying to spoil all her fun. Actually Fee was shooting me one of those too.

what was that about?

Then Soph gave out a squeal as she flipped to the next page of April's photo album, where she'd seen something, well, squeal-able.

I swivelled my head around and snuck a peek.

It was April with Cinderella (a lady dressed as Cinders, of course), with the cutest mini Cinderella standing by her side.

"Who's that?" I asked, pointing at the two-or-three-year-old little girl.

"Dunno," shrugged April. "Just some kid who snuck in the picture at the last minute."

"April! Could you put that away in your drawer, please?" Miss Levy suddenly called out.

April smiled sweetly at Miss Levy and then quickly turned the page.

"And this was taken when we got off the Pirates of the Caribbean ride. You'll never guess who shared our boat!"

"Who?" whispered Soph, her eyes as wide as could be.

"Only that guy from that boy band—"

"April! I don't want to have to ask you again!" called out Miss Levy.

"—that were number one all summer!" April carried on, in a voice that I think was supposed to be a whisper but wasn't quite.

"April!"

April shut her book quickly, and scurried over to her drawer, then scurried back again, with her head down.

For the rest of the morning, we did alliteration, which is that thing where loads of words in a sentence start with the same letter.

Miss Levy read us some poems and stuff that had a whole bunch of alliteration in them, then we had to do some examples of our own.

My favourite that I did was:

"Baby barn owls beating their wings in the bleak, black night."

I got the idea from Casper, of course, though he was beating his wings in our draughty garden shed, but there wasn't much alliteration in that.

Fee's was great, but then she is very good at big words. Hers was:

"The velociraptor vanished in the vastness of the velvet-blue vista."

Everyone in class liked that one, except Simon Green who made the **fart** nose again with his hands and got sent to Mr Ioannou.

Soph's was:

"Dancing and diving are things I definitely do,"

which worked, even if it wasn't as exciting as Fee's. (Maybe she should have added "with dinosaurs").

I wondered what April would come up with, but before Miss Levy got round to her, the bell **drinnnngggg-ed** for lunchtime.

"She did that deliberately!" I heard April mutter, as she, Soph and Fee squeezed and squashed out the door just ahead of me.

"Did what?" I asked the back of April's head.

"Miss Levy deliberately left me out then!" April sniffled, turning her head sideways on to answer me. "She doesn't like me! She's always picking on me!!"

I noticed Soph and Fee automatically snaking their arms around April.

But I couldn't feel sorry for her, 'cause I didn't think it was true. Miss Levy had been lovely to April so far this week. The only time she'd hassled her a little bit was earlier, when she wouldn't put her photo album away.

"It was only the Disneyland thing!" I said, in Miss Levy's defence.

uh-oh... Soph was frowning at me again. I think it was because I hadn't been very sympathetic to April. But why should I be when April was talking rubbish?

"I'm just going to ignore that," muttered April, staring down at the floor with a shrug.

What did she mean? Was she going to ignore whatever Miss Levy said to her? That was going to be **tricky**, since Miss Levy was our teacher, and we spent all day with her.

But Soph and Fee seemed to go along with what April was saying, from the way they were making agreeing sort of cooing noises.

I stayed silent now, thinking about April and her photo album, and felt – what was the right word? The one that means you don't quite believe something?

I'd've asked Fee, but I didn't want to explain why I needed to know, 'cause she'd think I was **n**ot being **n**ice to the **n**ew girl (hurray for the alliteration there!).

Oh, yeah; I remembered now – sceptical. I was sceptical about April's trip to Disneyland Paris, and the rides she was supposed to have gone on.

So I guess that made me **sceptical**, as well as **grumpy, confused, jealous, mean** and a **fibber**, of course.

(Oh, how I wished it was last week, before I told a stupid lie, and before April Joni Furneaux came to our school. Back then I was normal, boring and happy…)

Actually, I just realized something! Was April talking about ignoring Miss Levy there, or was she talking about ignoring me…?!

7

Three cheers
and a boo...

Last night, I dreamt that I was in the Mexican restaurant in the High Street.

Only everything was in a *muddle*; instead of being there with Soph and Fee and Soph's mum and dad, I was with Simon Green, Mrs O'Neill and Bart Simpson.

Instead of smiley waiters waving maracas, Simon and Bart were bashing each other over the head with them while Mrs O'Neill tutted a lot. And they were all ignoring me.

And there were no marshmallows on top of my ice-cream – only **yucky birdseed**...

When I woke up this morning, I didn't know what that dream meant, except that my brain had maybe turned to mush.

I nearly told Mum about my dream but…

a) I worried that she'd think I was trying to make her feel guilty about not letting me go to the restaurant.

b) She was eating her porridge very quietly outside in the shed, watching Casper to check if he was doing OK.

That was this morning. It was now 6.30pm on Friday evening, and somewhere on the High Street, Soph and Fee were probably starting on their marshmallow ice-creams and dancing in their seats to the sound of mariachi music. (Fee said that's Mexican music, with guitars and trumpets and maracas, of course.)

I wished I could hear mariachi music, but instead, I'd been listening to a CD of an opera singer called Placido Do-something, 'cause that happened to be Rose the rescue centre receptionist's favourite.

And it was her party, after all. Her leaving party.

But Mum had turned off Placido Do-something a couple of minutes ago to make a speech, and it was just about over.

"So can everyone raise their glasses…" said Mum with a smile.

(I'd finished my apple juice and left the cup somewhere, so I raised a handful of pretzels instead.)

"…and give three cheers for Rose! Hip, hip…"

Everybody in the reception of the Paws For Thought Animal Rescue Centre cheered, while several dogs joined in the best they could.

Rose looked very pleased to be surrounded by so many people (plus a few pets) at her leaving party.

And everyone looked very happy to be at the party, but sad to see her go, if the piles of presents and cards on her desk were anything to go by.

There were also piles of party food too, though Mum had put all the crisps and pizza and pretzels and stuff up high on shelves, to keep them out of **sniffing** and **scoffing** range of the four-legged party guests.

"Well, thank you, everyone!" Rose began, looking teary but happy. "I'd just like to say…"

While Rose gave a little speech in return, I put a smile on my face and pretended to listen. But really I was thinking about all the not-particularly-nice feelings that had been *swirling* around my head and chest all week.

And those feelings were…

1) The fibbing thing: I'd started to forget about that, till me and Mum left for the party tonight, and remembered with a sharp, unhappy ping why I wasn't with Soph and Fee instead.

2) The mean feeling: Not really liking April and not being able to figure out why.

3) The jealous feeling: At first that came when April described her mega-house, but now I was jealous because my friends were paying more attention to the new girl than to me.

4) The confused feeling: See number 2. And I was now also confused about whether April was talking about ignoring me or Miss Levy the other day.

5) The grumpy feeling: See number 3.

6) The sceptical feeling: It was all about April's Disneyland Paris trip. The Space Mountain thing to be precise.

Actually, I'd got a bit **obsessed** about the Space Mountain thing.

In fact, I phoned Dylan last night and asked if he could find out about the height restriction on that ride. Sure enough, he went on the Disney website and found out you had to be 1.32m to go on it.

Next, I went and found a tape measure (in the kitchen drawer alongside ringworm tablets and a leaflet on the life cycle of fleas) and measured myself.

I was 1.33m tall, and April was smaller than me by quite a lot. And she looked younger, and smaller still in the photos, so how could it be true that she went on Space Mountain?

Unless she was wearing platform trainers like Caitlin's, of course. But I'd never seen them for kids, specially not in Size Teeny-Tiny, which was what April must be…

"Indie?"

That was Mum's voice. I suddenly realized that…

a) Mum had already said my name quite a few times.

b) Placido Do-something was warbling again.

c) I was still holding my pretzels in the air.

"Mmm?" I mumbled, wondering who the man was with Mum. He was trying to coax Ed the very shy parrot off Mum's shoulder and didn't seem to be bothered that he was getting his finger nipped for his trouble.

"Indie, this is Arthur," said Mum, nodding her head towards the man Ed was biting. With a grown-up name like that and his black-rimmed glasses, Arthur seemed like the sort of person you'd see on the TV news, reporting on the economic state of the EU, or explaining what the

space-time continuum

was, or other things I wouldn't understand, even if I lived to be a hundred and twelve.

"Hello," I said in my **best(est)**, **polite(est)** voice, then took a nibble of a party pretzel.

"Arthur's going to be our new receptionist!" said Mum.

"BUT... crkk..." I choked on my pretzel. "He can't be - he's a man!!"

As soon as I said it, I spotted the surprised looks on Mum, Rose and Arthur's faces.

OOPS... I hadn't meant it that way, but I guess it sounded like a man should never do a job like a receptionist's. And that maybe being a receptionist was a rubbish job.

Urgh. Now I coming across all rude, as well as all that other stuff.

Boo...

Goofball is good

I felt like hugging Arthur the new receptionist at the party yesterday, mainly 'cause he burst out laughing at me.

OK, so normally it's not fantastic to have someone burst out laughing at you. But with Arthur laughing, everyone else had started laughing, so it seemed more like I'd said something kind of **goofball-y** instead of downright rude.

Goofball was good. I mean, it was much better that everyone thought I was a **goofball** than the rude person I knew I'd sounded like.

By the way, when I say everyone was laughing, I think I'd say that Mum was more smiling at me in a confused way. I think what was going through her head was: "Who is this **fibbing, rude** girl who's impersonating my usually nice daughter?"

She didn't mention it to me when we got home though. Mainly because she was in the shed most of the time, fretting over Casper, who'd gone off his diet of worms. **(Blee...)**

Anyway, never mind all of that rude/ goofball/wormy stuff.

You know how I said my step-mum Fiona was fine?

Well, what wasn't so fine was spending Saturday afternoon in a garden centre, schlepping around after her as she compared lawn trimmers and studied deciduous shrubs or whatever.

I was here because Caitlin wasn't back from her holiday till tomorrow, and Mum had to do a shift at the Rescue Centre.

And Dad couldn't look after me, 'cause Saturday is his busiest work day – he had five weddings to photograph.

(Honestly, he can be as *ditzy* as Mum sometimes. I saw a note in his kitchen about his 1pm wedding. It said:

CHURCH: Gavin Thompson
BRIDE: Tracey Hutchings
GROOM: St Peter-in-the-Fields

I hope Dad got there OK – the Gavin Thomson church won't have been on any map. And the bride might be *puzzled* to find herself marrying a hundred-and-fifty-year-old building…)

"What's this?" Dylan suddenly asked me, holding up a very small tree, which was as tall as a hamster standing on its back legs.

"It's a bonsai. It's like a real tree but in miniature."

"Why?" asked Dylan.

Dylan asks the sort of questions that

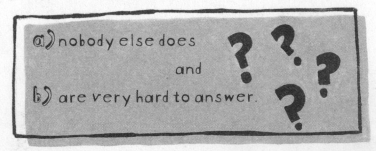

a) nobody else does
            and
b) are very hard to answer.

"Just because…" I mumbled, realising that I sounded like a grumpy mum with a toddler in the endless 'but why, mummy?' stage.

I decided to pretend I was hugely interested in the cacti, in the hope he'd stop talking for a little bit. I do like Dylan loads, but like Marmite or a family-size bag of salt-and-vinegar crisps, you can only take so much of him.

I mean, he'd already fried my brain with questions like these…

- "Why do people want water features in their gardens?"
(Because people like the sound of water.)
- "Why don't they live beside a stream, then?"
(Because not everyone

can live beside
streams.)

• "Why don't they just
turn their taps on, and
listen to that instead?"

(Pretended I didn't hear that one
and hid behind some deciduous shrubs.)

• "Can you see any Venus Fly-Traps?"
(Argh, he found me. No I couldn't.)

• "Do you know how Venus Fly-Traps
digest the flies they catch?"
(No. But Dylan did, and gave me a very
looooonnnnggg explanation.)

• "Do you know which flies Venus Fly-
Traps prefer?"

(No, Dylan guessed bluebottles,
since they'd be like the McDonald's
Mega-Whopper or whatever of
the fly world.)

• "What is that funny blue food for slugs?"

(It kills them, Dylan.)

I thought I might die of irritation if Dylan carried on with any more gardening-related questions.

"**ouch!**" yelped Dylan, sidling up to me and stroking a cactus for no good reason. "What's the point of these stupid prickles?!!"

To stop stupid nine-year-old boys stroking them, I nearly said.

"To stop animals from eating them," I really said.

"So why don't plants like daisies and daffodils have spikes?"

Instead of coming up with a reply (ie, saying, "Just because…" again), I got lost in thoughts of cacti growing wild and free in Mexico (instead of small and in loudly painted pots in the Sunshine Garden Centre).

Which in turn got me thinking about Mexican food.

Which got me thinking how the meal went last night.

"How's the alien?" Dylan asked out of the blue, as he tried to pick a tricky prickle out of his finger.

"Excuse me?"

"That new alien girl in your class. Have you caught her talking in her own alien language yet? Or seen her doing anything suspicious, like accidentally let her tentacles show?"

OK, so that was pretty funny.

But having April Joni Furneaux in my class wasn't very funny.

The more she talked, the less my friends seemed to notice to me. Maybe they were all trying to ignore the things I said now, not just April.

Or was I making it all up and getting paranoid?

There was only one way to find out if everything was normal and OK between me and my two best mates.

I'd phone Soph right now and ask how the meal went.

The only trouble was, I was only meant to use my mobile in emergencies, so it didn't fry my brain. Although it already felt frazzled.

I glanced around and spotted my step-mum, stroking some paving stones.

Fiona! I'm just going to the loo!

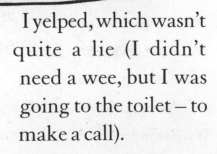

I yelped, which wasn't quite a lie (I didn't need a wee, but I was going to the toilet – to make a call).

Yelping that out loud was a bit stupid, I realized, as I slunk off – red-faced – past lots of grinning garden centre customers, who sadly weren't deaf.

"Hello?" said Soph.

"Soph, it's me!" I said, sitting on the lid of a toilet at the far end of the garden centre. "How was the Mexican restaurant?"

The best answer she could have given me was that at the last minute, she and Fee had persuaded her parents to postpone the meal to a day where I could come.

Instead, I got the **worst** answer.

"Oh, it was great! We ate so much we thought we'd explode!" (So far, so friendly.) "Y'know April said–"

"April?" I interrupted. Why was April's name coming up in Soph's story about the Mexican restaurant?

"Oh, um, yeah!" muttered Soph, sounding awkward. "Fee thought it would be cool to invite her along, since you couldn't come."

Another thing I couldn't do was speak. Or gulp. There was some kind of big knot in my throat.

"We, um,

just felt so sorry for her," Soph babbled on. "After you left school yesterday, she burst out crying and said that her step-mum had banned photos of her real mum from around the house!"

Yikes. That sounded awful.

But being treated like your feelings didn't matter to your friends felt a little bit awful too.

"Oh. R-really?" I mumbled and coughed, trying to move the knot in my throat. "Listen, I've got to go – my step-mum wants me. See you Monday…"

See all that stuff about me being **rude** and **sceptical** and **grumpy** and **confused** and **mean** and a **fibber?**

Well, to that list you can add **hurt**, big-time…

9

Welcome back, Caitlin!

"Hey, kid!!"
I hadn't realized quite how much I'd missed Caitlin till she came barging in the front door on Sunday morning with seventy-five bags (nearly) and a *strange* new haircut.

(I quite liked the *weird* shape but I wasn't keen on the yellow fringe.)

"How was the bus journey?" I asked, watching as she dumped her seventy-five bags (nearly) in a pile that the dogs immediately started scrambling over.

"**Terrible!**" laughed Caitlin, pulling one plastic bag out of the pile that the dogs seemed very **sniffily** interested in. "Seven hours with no sleep!"

You could tell. She had purply circles of tiredness around her eyes, which toned rather nicely with her purple tartan mini-kilt.

"But was it lovely to see your family and your friends?" I asked, following Caitlin through to the kitchen.

She plonked the plastic bag on the table and tipped out the contents.

"Yeah – specially my mum," Caitlin smiled, sitting down and kicking off her heavy black biker boots.

(Dibbles scurried under the table, lifted one of them in his mouth and took it away somewhere to **sniff**. Maybe he could pick up exciting scents of Scotland. Or maybe just the smell of the overnight National Express coach.)

"Look at this bag of stuff my mum put together for me!" said Caitlin, spreading out an array of snacks that looked like they'd make serious nutritionist people faint with shock.

There was normal shortbread and millionaires' shortbread (with gooey toffee and chocolate layers), some kind of squashed, flat rolls covered in sugar ('rowies', apparently), macaroni cheese pies, tablet (hard, sugary chunks of deliciousness) and – best of all – Tunnocks Tea Cakes.

Mmmm, marshmallow-y, chocolate-y, biscuit-y things of yummy-ness.

But then the thought of marshmallows gave me a sudden sharp, hurt ping. Oh, those Mexican marshmallows being eaten on Friday by someone who wasn't me…

Caitlin didn't seem to notice my ping. Maybe it was because she was too busy shooing dogs' noses from the edge of the table.

"Where's your mum?" she asked, as she shooed.

"Out in the shed. She's got some sick baby barn owl in there."

As soon as I spoke, Caitlin stopped shooing and shot me a look.

"What?" I said.

"Why did you say 'some sick baby barn barn owl'?" Caitlin quizzed me.

"Uh, 'cause that's what it is?" I answered warily.

"Yeah, but it's the way you said it. All casual, like it wasn't important!"

oooh, had I really sounded like that? Like I didn't really care too much about Casper?

Same as Mum, I cared madly about all animals. Usually.

"Well, I…" I mumbled, trying to figure out why I wasn't wild about Casper.

Then – **blam!** – it suddenly came to me.

Every time I'd peeked in the garden shed window at the little barn owl this week, it had reminded me of a certain small-ish, blonde-ish, odd-ish girl, and made my heart sink.

It wasn't its fault, the poor baby barn owl…

"What?" asked Caitlin, fixing me with a question that sounded as odd as one of Dylan's.

"What what?" I answered, my head still reeling from realising why I hadn't fallen for Casper.

"What's going on with you?" said Caitlin, more to the point.

OK, it was time to tell, and Caitlin was just the right person. She was a girl, and she'd only been out of school a couple of years. Maybe she'd help me figure out what it was about April Joni Furneaux that bugged me, and what it was about April Joni Furneaux that made my best friends so crazy about her.

So I told her everything.

I told her lots of random stuff about April.

Like about her **scary peanut allergy** and her **huge house** and her **huger bedroom** and how a **sting-ray** once bit her and how her dad looked like **George Clooney** and about her **wicked step-mother** who only spoke to her through bossy, mean notes and about her **evil, spoilt step-sister** and how she once shared a boat with the singer of a **boy band** on the Pirates of the Caribbean ride at Disneyland Paris and how she went on **Space Mountain,** only I didn't see how she could have, and how she seemed to like my **two best friends** an awful lot, and how I was pretty sure she'd said something to Soph and Fee about **ignoring me**...

When I finished, I realized that Caitlin had eaten three of the six Tunnock's Tea Cakes in the packet while she was listening, so I'd better hurry and catch up with her.

"Wewl, it'ch obviush, ishn't it?" said Caitlin through a mouthful of delicious, sticky gloop.

"What is?" I asked, before I bit into my own chunk of delicious, sticky gloop.

Caitlin took a gulp, wiped her sticky fingers on her mini-kilt, and made her pronouncement.

"She's lying, isn't she?"

"Is she?" I gasped. How could Caitlin sound so sure?

"Of course!" shrugged Caitlin, as if it was as obvious as, well, a very obvious thing.

"But how do you know?" I frowned at her.

"'Cause I went through a phase of lying like that once when I started at a new school and was dead nervous and scared," said Caitlin. "I talked too much and told stories to impress people or make them feel sorry for me, just so I could get friends."

"Did you? Like what?"

"Oh, the best one was that my uncle worked in a crisp factory and sent me heaps of free crisps," said Caitlin, laughing at the memory.

"Did your friends find out you were lying?"

"No. I just had to spend all my pocket money on crisps for the next two years, so I could hand them out to my mates. That taught me not to lie again!"

I listened as Caitlin told me more, but my brain was silently chattering to me.

It was helping me figure out that I'd thought all along that April's stories might be lies – but had felt mean thinking that of her.

"And the thing is, you might be right about her blanking you, kid," Caitlin carried on. "'Cause I bet April sort of suspects you might know she's lying."

As I nodded at Caitlin's chatter and took another bite of Tea Cake, I realized that – for the first time in a week – I had a lovely new feeling in my chest... **relief.**

Phew, I wasn't all **mean** and **rude** and the rest.

And – hey – I wasn't the only fibber around...

10

Sort of sorry

With April on my mind, I went out and collected slugs this morning.

OK, let me explain: I wasn't about to do anything mean like smuggle them into school and stuff them in April's pencil case.

It was just that after talking to Caitlin, I felt like I understood April a bit more and also felt sort of sorry for her.

After all, I'd slipped into telling a lie

pretty easily, so maybe April had started with just one, harmless little white lie, and then she got so much attention that she told another one, and another one, till she'd found herself stuck in the middle of a giant lie snowball.

And since I was thinking **nicer, fluffier** thoughts about April, I started thinking **nicer, fluffier** thoughts about the poor, little, fluffy baby barn owl out in the shed.

Mum had been feeding Casper with chopped up worms in some kind of warm vitamin gloop that the vet had given her (mmm, delicious!). But he'd gone right off it, and was on hunger strike. Which isn't good for anyone, but specially not good for baby barn owls that aren't old enough to go out and find their own food in the wild.

Mum was worried, I knew, because she'd forgotten to eat both her tea last night (who could forget to eat spaghetti bolognese?) and her breakfast this morning (bran flakes, but she forgot to pour any milk in).

Suddenly, while I was eating my own breakfast cereal, I had a **brainwave** and made a plan: one that involved crawling around in the garden with a small plastic tub, and three dogs sniffing alongside me, wondering what I was doing.

What I was doing was gathering a few fat slugs, to see if I could tempt Casper to eat.

Since Mum was already in the shed with Casper, and I knew not to interrupt them, I left the slug tub outside the shed with a note for Mum to find.

Hi Casper!

Thought you might like these. They're like wine gums for owls. Hope you're healthy and hooting again soon.

Love,
Indie xxx

(I had thought about leaving the note and the slug tub in the kitchen, but Mum could be so *dippy* I worried she'd miss the note and I'd find the slug tub put away in the fridge beside my strawberry yoghurts.)

Anyway, I was dying to get to school.

I was dying to get hold of Soph and Fee and tell them what I (OK, Caitlin) had sussed out about April.

And I didn't have long to wait; there they were, just about to amble through the school gate!

Before I told them anything, I wanted to show them I was their **happy, upbeat** friend, and not all miserable about missing the Mexican meal on Friday, or flipped out about them inviting April along instead. (Even if I was, just a little bit.)

I hurtled towards them, barging in between and flinging my arms around their shoulders.

"Indie! You gave me a scare!" **giggled** Soph.

"You noodle! I nearly had a heart attack!" Fee laughed and gasped.

Yay! Everything was normal and **lovely** and **jokey** with my **best(est)** friends.

Drinnnnnnnnnggggggggggg!!!! Went the school bell.

"Listen, I've got to tell you something!" I said urgently, holding them back from walking towards the main entrance.

"What?" asked Soph, while Fee just frowned.

"well, I think April is a liar!" I blurted out with a big smile.

OopS. That came out all clunky.

Same as Friday, when I'd said Arthur couldn't be a receptionist 'cause he was a man.

What I'd *meant* to say was, 'Caitlin thinks that maybe April has been feeling ultra-nervous starting at a new school and that maybe, possibly, she's done a bunch of exaggerating and possibly told a few little white lies to get our attention.'

Yep, that would have been a lot better than blurting out "April is a liar!"

In the deadly silence of the second after I spoke, I saw Soph look at Fee and Fee look at Soph.

Soph's eyes were wide, and Fee's were narrow.

Fee turned her narrowed eyes to me, while Soph made her wide eyes stare at the ground.

"April told us you'd say that," said Fee.

"What? She told you I'd say she was a liar?!" I repeated, confused.

Was April a mind-reader as well as a fibber?

"Well, not that she was a liar, exactly," said Fee, "but she warned us you'd say nasty things about her to us. And she was right!"

Urgh... no wonder my best friends hadn't felt so friendly lately!

"She said you were **jealous** 'cause we liked her," muttered Soph, in an awkward-sounding voice. "She said you'd been a little bit mean to her too."

"I haven't been mean to her!" I said, in a hurt **squeak**.

"She says you keep giving her dirty looks," Fee added. "And you tut at her all the time."

What? I tutted at her? When?!

"But you've both been with me whenever I've been near April! Have you ever heard me tutting?"

"She says you do it when we can't hear," said Fee, all matter-of-fact.

"Oh, she's such a liar!!" I spluttered, before I burst at the unfairness of it all.

"Indie!" gasped Fee. "How can you be so horrible about someone who's had such a hard time?"

"Yeah, she's got a horrible step-mum and nut allergy and everything!" Soph chipped in.

Before I could say anything else (which I couldn't, I was so stunned), my two not-best-friends-anymore stomped away from me, towards the doors and sound of the **DRINGGGGGG-INGGGGG!!!** bell.

I felt suddenly sicker than a barn owl that had gone off its worm gloop…

11

Ignored at close quarters

Being ignored by someone is not nice.

Being ignored by three someones is triple not nice.

It was lucky for me that this Monday was the sort of day at school where there wasn't much sitting-at-your-table time. (Hurray for assembly and PE and doing a messy art project and having a talk from a policeman about road safety.)

Sitting-at-the-table time would have made the whole day super-uncomfortable, what with being ignored at close quarters by Soph, Fee and April.

To help me ignore being ignored at breaktimes, I went and helped tangle up the five-year-olds in their skipping ropes.

And at lunchtime, I sat with Georgia Jones and Ayse Keçeli, which would have been quite a nice change if it hadn't been for the fact that Soph, Fee and April were sitting at the next table ignoring me.

Oh, and for the fact that Simon Green was sitting opposite me, Georgia and Ayse, sticking chips up his nose and then eating them.

But at last – with the end-of-day bell – my long, endless day of being ignored was over.

(I was trying not to think about the fact that I might get ignored the next day too. Or all week. Or for the rest of my time at primary school.)

Right now, I could see Soph, Fee and April up ahead of me in the playground, walking towards the big crowd of hanging-around parents.

They were walking slowly, but I was walking slower, since I didn't fancy catching them up and being ignored for one last time today.

Yay! Then I saw exactly what I needed
to cheer me up – Caitlin!

"Hey, kid!!" she yelled, smiling and
waving madly.

The mums and dads and childminders
round about her stared and backed away
slightly. Not just because she'd bellowed
so loudly, but because she was dressed
pretty loudly too.

She was like a fashion experiment gone wrong. But she didn't care that her yellow fringe didn't match her red long-sleeved T-shirt or her purple tartan mini or her blue over-the-knee socks or her pink platform trainers.

She was like a bright peacock in amongst lots of beige hamsters, and I was so proud of her.

Just as I was waving back, I noticed the a pretty little kid come hurtling out of the waiting mum-crowd. She was about three, and looked kind of familiar.

Where had I seen her before? The park? The nursery attached to the school? Was she one of the vets' kids from the rescue centre?

She was Disney cute, with huge blue eyes and blonde hair. She –

Wait a minute… she was the mini Cinderella in April's photo from Disneyland Paris!

And she was squealing, "April! April! April!!" at the top of her teeny voice, as she hurtled herself at April Joni Furneaux's knees and hugged on tight.

Er… so that little girl in April's photo wasn't some random kid who'd wandered into the shot? She was April's horrible, spoilt brat step-sister, wasn't she? A horrible, spoilt brat of a step-sister who was now staring up at April adoringly. **Hmm…**

I was pretty close behind April, Soph and Fee now, and could hear what April said next.

"Daisy! What are you doing here? Where's Carla?"

"Mummy's over there!" said the little girl,

nodding her head in the direction of a **smiley, cuddly** lady walking towards them.

"April! Surprise! Managed to get off work early to pick you up!!" said the woman who was April's wicked stepmother, though she didn't look very wicked. Not the way she was waving that big bag of Maltesers in the air. "And look, I got your favourites!"

Standing practically right behind my old best friends now, I noticed:

1. Soph and Fee staring at the person we'd all thought was Cruella De Vil's less-nice-relation
2. Soph and Fee staring at each other
3. Soph and Fee staring at April
4. April blinking at Soph and Fee
5. April bursting into tears and running off at high speed, which was very hard to do with a small girl attached to her knees...

12

Getting-caught-fibbing-itis

Miss Levy was wrestling with a window that didn't want to open.

Which gave me and Soph and Fee a few precious moments to yak before register time.

"Where do you think she is?" Soph asked in a hushed voice.

We all stared at April's very empty seat.

"She's got to be feeling terrible," whispered Fee.

"Yes, but you can't stay off school with getting-caught-fibbing-itis," I pointed out.

I felt **bad** that April might be feeling bad this morning.

But I felt **very, very good** to be best friends with my best friends again.

We'd started to make up about three seconds after April ran out of the playground yesterday, once it had dawned on Soph and Fee that maybe April hadn't been telling the truth about stuff after all, and I hadn't been just a great big jealous meanie either.

We'd made up completely by the time we'd finished the ice-creams that Caitlin had bought for us all.

("Ice-cream is very good for shock," she'd told us wisely, as she queued at the van parked outside of school. I think that might have been a lie too, but a **very delicious** one.)

"But why would she tell us all those stories?" Fee had asked Caitlin. I think she was so startled by what had just happened that she forgot to be startled by Caitlin's new hairdo.

"Because she wanted you to like her. So sometimes she told you stuff to impress you, or so you'd feel sorry for her," Caitlin explained, same as she'd done for me the day before, over Tunnocks Tea Cakes.

"Hey, maybe she's gone back to her old school!" Soph now suggested, nodding at the empty seat next to her.

"Maybe!" Fee agreed.

"Should we ask Miss Levy?" I wondered, watching our teacher as she wrestled the window.

But we weren't able to ask Miss Levy straight away. Mrs Nicholl from the school office had just come in and was having one of those grown-up **whisper-y** conversations that adults at school sometimes have. They usually looked very important, as if they're saying stuff like, "Should we do a school swap, and trade Simon Green for a nice boy from Alaska?"

"Indie! And the Sophies! Could you go to Mr Ioannou's office, please?" said Miss Levy suddenly, as Mrs Nicholls slipped out of the door.

Eeeeek!!

Why were we being sent to Mr Ioannou's office?

Miss Levy was smiling, but in a strangely serious way, so that didn't give us any clues.

As we nervously got up and left the classroom, Simon Green did one of those **"WOOOOO-OOOOO-OOOh!"** things that's like short-hand for "boy-oh-boy, you're in trouble!"

"What have we done?" gulped Soph, when we got out into the long, echoing corridor.

"Oh, no – is it because of the nail varnish?!" fretted Fee.

Help! We all looked in a panic at our purple nails, which Caitlin had done for us when we hung out at mine after school yesterday.

'No nail varnish' was yet another rule on our list of school rules.

"We'll just have to keep our hands in our pockets or behind our backs!" I told the other two.

Caitlin had been brilliant at getting us to bond yesterday. She'd got Soph and Fee to phone their parents and ask to stay for tea. She'd made a mountain of fish fingers (only slightly burned) with half a bottle of tomato sauce on top, and played us our favourite songs on her didgeridoo.

She'd taken us outside to peek in the garden shed, and surprised me with the great news that Casper was better and had started eating again (yay for slug wine gums!). She'd put face packs on us and painted our fingernails purple and our toenails neon green, and it had been **excellent**.

It wasn't so **excellent** that we'd all forgotten to take off the purple nail varnish and were going to be punished for it, though…

We were outside Mr Ioannou's office now, and all too scared to knock. Perhaps he heard our hearts beating, because next thing, the door was pulled open.

"Hello, girls! Come on in," said Mr Ioannou, using a friendly-but-at-the-same-time-serious voice.

"Thank you," we all mumbled in minute voices, clenching our hands tight, with nails tucked out of sight.

Then all our mouths turned into startled 'o's.

'Cause there in Mr Ioannou's office was April (sniffling into a tissue), the Malteser-waving woman from yesterday, and a tall, bald man with quite big ears.

"Indie, Sophie, Sophie... you know April. Well, this is her father and step-mum," said Mr Ioannou, introducing us to people who didn't look at all like either Cruella De Vil or George Clooney.

Me, Soph and Fee nervously sat down where Mr Ioannou was pointing.

urgh... a panicky thought had just pinged in my head.

Had April been lying again? Had she maybe told her parents and Mr Ioannou that we'd been bullying her or something?

My brain suddenly started *swirling* with worry, and I nearly missed what our headteacher was saying.

"…has got herself in a bit of a pickle," Mr Ioannou was explaining, in quite a kindly voice. "She wants to say sorry to you for not quite telling the truth about many things."

At that, April started sobbing into her tissue, while her 'evil' step-mother gave her a **lovely cuddle**.

"Girls, it's been a hard time for April," said the man who looked about as much like a movie star as I looked like a giraffe. "Her mum remarried and moved to Wales a few months ago, so she hasn't been able to see her as much as she'd like."

Ooh, that must be hard, I thought, remembering how lucky I was to see Dad every Sunday and sometimes other days too. And how hard it was for my step-brother Dylan, whose dad lived all the way away in Tasmania.

"And two rather silly girls at her old school–"

"Ria and Terri-Ann," April's step-mum interrupted her husband.

"–yes, Ria and Terri-Ann, well, they started bullying her about her not having a mother. It got so upsetting for April that we decided it would be best to swap schools."

Wow, so at least that bit was true. And awful.

"Anyway, I think that April may have told you girls some stories, just to win your friendship," continued Mr Ioannou, "and she knows it was wrong, and she'd like to say sorry to you all."

Especially me, I thought, since April's fibs hadn't been about winning my friendship, but stealing my friends…

"Especially you, Indie, because she knows some of the things she said might have been hurtful to you," Mr Ioannou added.

In the little bubble of silence that followed, April lifted her blonde head, looked at us with watery eyes and **snivelled** a wibbly **"sorry!!"** at us all.

"Do you girls have anything to say?" asked our headteacher.

"So... um..." began Fee, staring at April, "you don't really have a nut allergy?"

"Uh-uh," answered April, in the smallest voice possible.

"And you don't have a huge house with a bedroom big enough for six people to sleep over and a pink fridge?" asked Soph.

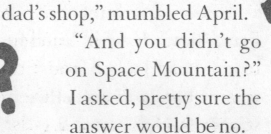

"We live in a flat above my dad's shop," mumbled April.

"And you didn't go on Space Mountain?" I asked, pretty sure the answer would be no.

"No."

"Have you really been on the London Eye six times?" Fee checked.

"No."

"Did a stingray once bite you?" Soph asked next.

"No."

None of us said anything about stuff like being on the Pirates of the Carribbean ride with the lead singer of a boy band, or if her step-mum really banned photos of her real mum, 'cause we knew what the answer would be.

"These are three very good, helpful and thoughtful students, Mr and Mr Furneaux," said Mr Ioannou, motioning towards me, Soph and Fee. "I'm sure they're happy to accept the apology, and start over. How about it, girls?"

Still stunned, and sitting in a row like baby barn owls on a branch, we said nothing at first.

Then I remembered the birdseed and poor, flu-y Mrs O'Neill and sad, starving Archie the budgie, and I knew what I had to do.

"Of course we'll start over!" I said.

Soph and Fee nodded along with my words.

And immediately, April and her parents gave us all smiles that were so grateful, it was as if we'd just told them they'd won the lottery.

It was a pretty fantastic feeling to make people look that **happy**.

And it made me kind of **giddy** to have a **fantastic** feeling after last week, when all I felt was **mean** and **rude** and **grumpy** and the rest.

It made me want to **giggle** and **laugh**, and maybe spin April around till she stopped feeling guilty and started **giggling** too!

It made me want to give her the Tunnocks Tea Cake that I'd smuggled into school in my coat pocket!!

Er, wait a minute.

Maybe that was going a bit too far.

I mean, I was definitely, one hundred percent going to give April a chance to start over being our friend, but there was no need to give her my Tunnock's Tea Cake, since it was my new favourite and it was my last one.

Maybe – if you're being **ultra-good** in other ways – it's OK to be a little bit selfish sometimes…?